A Shipful of Shivers

By Diane Muldrow
Illustrated by Chris Nowell

©1995, 1996, 1998 Nintendo, CREATURES, GAME FREAK. ™ & ®
are trademarks of Nintendo. ©2000 Nintendo. All Rights Reserved.

GOLDEN BOOKS®, A GOLDEN BOOK®, and G DESIGN®
are trademarks of Golden Books Publishing Company, Inc.

A GOLDEN BOOK®
Golden Books Publishing Company, Inc.
New York, New York 10106

Library of Congress Catalog Card Number: 00-103118
ISBN: 0-307-16904-9   MM

It was a beautiful day to be on the water. Ash, Misty, Tracey, Pikachu, and Togepi were excited to reach Moro Island, as they continued their Orange Island adventures.

Ash contacted Professor Oak as soon as they landed.

"How are ya, Professor? We're on Moro Island!" announced Ash.

"Aaahh . . . you timed your arrival perfectly!" said the professor.

"Divers have just recovered a three-hundred-year-old Orange Island League championship trophy. It was found on a sunken ship, off the coast of Moro Island."

Ash, Misty, and Tracey couldn't wait to visit the museum where the trophy was displayed.

But an unpleasant surprise awaited the friends at the museum doors.

Officer Jenny announced, "The old Orange Island League trophy we had on display here has been stolen!"

The disappointed friends turned away with the rest of the crowd.

"I really wanted to see that old championship trophy from the Orange Island League," said Ash.

Just then, the friends bumped into Team Rocket, waking up in the bushes outside the museum. They heard Meowth yawn and say, "There's nothin' like wakin' up after a good night's heist!"

"A heist?" cried Misty.

Team Rocket panicked. They'd been found out!

"W-w-we don't know anything about any championship trophies," said Meowth.

James pushed Meowth aside with a nervous laugh, and said, "A-a-and if we did, a stolen one certainly wouldn't be in this package!"

With that, Team Rocket took off.

With Ash and his friends close behind, Team Rocket ran with the heavy trophy to the water's edge.

"Look! There's a boat we can swipe!" cried Meowth.

Team Rocket jumped onto a pedal boat that looked like Seadra and began to pedal as fast as they could.

"Team Rocket is getting away with the trophy!" Misty cried.

Ash wasted no time.
"Lapras, I choose you!" he yelled, hurling a Poké Ball.

"Lapras, follow that boat!" shouted Ash.
There was no time to lose!

Meanwhile, James was out of breath. "We . . . can't pedal this thing . . . fast enough," he panted. "They'll catch us any second now!"

Meowth frowned and said, "We won't go any faster with you flappin' your gums!"

That's when Team Rocket realized that the sun had gone away. They were surrounded by fog.

"Perfect!" said Meowth. "Those kids'll never spot us in this soup!"

Suddenly, something large loomed over Team Rocket— something very, very large.

"Look! A ship," said Jessie.

James looked up at the creaking old ship with tattered sails. "It looks abandoned," he observed.

Team Rocket pedaled over to the ship's ladder and climbed aboard. The ship was perfectly quiet.

"Nobody here but Team Rocket!" said Meowth with a wicked laugh.

"This is the perfect place to hide out!" cried Jessie.

But Team Rocket wasn't really alone . . . they were being watched overhead by a ghost!

"Aaaaaaagggghhhhh!" they cried, noticing the ghost above them. They ran away as fast as they could—so fast that they tore a hole in the deck and fell down, down into the ship's dark hold.

Just as Ash and his friends were beginning to think they'd lost Team Rocket, they discovered the ship—and Team Rocket's boat alongside.

"Come on!" said Ash. "We'll have to get on that old ship! It must be the ship the divers raised. The one that had the Orange Island trophy on board!"

Misty climbed up the ladder with her friends, but she had a weird feeling about being on the creepy old ship.

Suddenly, a mast snapped and crashed behind her! As Misty hurled herself forward, little Togepi flew out of her arms toward the deep, black hole in the deck.

"Pi-ka-CHU!" cried Pikachu, jumping to catch Togepi. But Pikachu wasn't fast enough and Togepi fell down into the darkness.

Togepi wasn't hurt at all. It got right up and began to explore the ship.

Elsewhere down below, Team Rocket was still being scared silly. A ghost grabbed the bag containing the trophy. What could Jessie and James do now?

While Team Rocket was trying to hold onto the trophy, Misty and her friends searched for Togepi. Finally they found it, giggling with two ghosts!

"Togepi, thank goodness you're safe!" cried Misty. Then she got angry. "You'd better leave my Togepi alone," she shouted at the ghosts. "Go, Staryu!"

With a screech, Staryu flew out of its Poké Ball toward the ghosts. As it scooped off their sheets, Ash and his friends gasped.

"It's Gastly and Haunter!" said Tracey.

Ash pulled out his Pokédex. "Gastly, the Gas Pokémon," announced the mechanical voice of Dexter. "Haunter, the Gas Pokémon: After evolving from Gastly, this Haunter can learn the Dream Eater and Psychic attacks."

As the friends watched, the two Pokémon played with Togepi and made it laugh. They weren't trying to hurt little Togepi at all.

Then the friends noticed something else—the Orange Island Trophy! Gastly and Haunter quickly flew over to it, and guarded it.

"That trophy belongs in the museum, and we're taking it back!" cried Ash.

Just then, Team Rocket appeared. "Oh, yeah?" said Meowth. "That's what you think, twerpy!"

"Victreebel, go!" cried James. A Pokémon battle was on! Victreebel sent out its Razor Leaf Attack. But the sharp, shooting leaves did nothing to harm Gastly.

"Arbok! Tackle Attack!" ordered Jessie. Arbok lunged toward Haunter—and went right through it! Chuckling, Haunter used its Confuse Ray Attack on Arbok, who turned and attacked Team Rocket! Victreebel was down, too.

Then Meowth spoke. "We are Gastly and Haunter," it said.

"Hey," said Misty, "what's Meowth talking about?"

"Haunter must be controlling Meowth somehow so it can speak to us!" replied Tracey. Haunter had put all of Team Rocket in a trance.

"For centuries, we've guarded this Orange Island League championship trophy," said Gastly and Haunter. "Our master was captain of this ship. He loved Pokémon, and especially prized us. One night, we were caught in a terrible storm, and our ship sunk to the bottom of the sea. A few days ago, humans came and took our master's prized possession. So we raised the ship, and went in search of our captain's treasure.

"Our captain was a fine Pokémon trainer, and we were proud to help win the championship," continued Haunter and Gastly. "We hope you will understand why we can never allow anyone to take this trophy."

"Sure," agreed Ash. "Just because the captain isn't around anymore doesn't mean the trophy shouldn't still be his!"

"Now the time has come for you to leave this place," said Haunter and Gastly.

Just then, Jessie, James, and Meowth woke up from their trance and demanded the trophy. Pikachu took control of the situation and gave them an electric shock they never forgot! Team Rocket was blasting off again!

Gastly and Haunter said good-bye, then they began to raise their ship once more.

The friends watched in awe as the ship rose up in the air high above them.

"I guess they must be taking the ship to a place where no one can find it," said Tracey.

Misty nodded. "I sure hope so," she whispered.

"Bye, Gastly! Bye Haunter!" called Ash. "Take care of that trophy!"

The ship went higher and higher until it was only a tiny speck against the full moon. The friends smiled, knowing the captain's prized trophy was safe forever.